CINDERELLA

from the opera by Gioacchino Rossini in a version

written and illustrated by

BENI MONTRESOR

Alfred A. Knopf · New York

4777

This title was originally catalogued by the Library of Congress as follows:

MONTRESOR, BENI
Cinderella.
    Cinderella. From the opera by Gioacchino Rossini in a
version written and illustrated by Beni Montresor. New
York. Knopf [1965]
        1 v. (unpaged)   col. illus.   21 x 26 cm.

    I. Rossini, Gioacchino Antonio, 1792–1868. La Cenerentola.
II. Montresor, Beni.

PZ8.C488Mo   65—21556

Library of Congress   [66k4]

Trade Ed.: ISBN: 0- 394-81055-4 — Lib. Ed.: ISBN: 0- 394-91055-9

To Nin, with lilies and roses

In the ancient city of Montefiascone, there stood the castle of the Baron of Montefiascone. The castle had once been magnificent but now was falling to pieces, all because the Baron thought only of his own pleasure.

The Baron's two daughters, Tisbe and Clorinda, were just like him. They were frivolous and vain and squandered money on jewels, furs, and fine clothes.

There came a day when the Baron's fortune was all gone. What to do now? The scheming Baron was not long without a solution. He would marry a rich widow, the mother of gentle Angelina.

The castle again was filled to overflowing and the eating and dancing went on for weeks on end. When they had finished, the Baron was as poor as before.

Angelina's mother died of a broken heart, leaving her daughter to the mercy of Tisbe and Clorinda.

They put her to work in the kitchen making her slave day and night. Because her only dress was soon covered with ashes, they called her Cinderella.

One fine morning, there was a knock at the kitchen door and a strange beggar entered.

"Have pity on the poor," he said, and gentle Cinderella brought him some bread.

When Tisbe and Clorinda saw this, they flew into a rage and began to beat both the beggar and Cinderella.

The beggar fled. As he vanished through the door, he called back mysteriously, "Foolish girls, if only you knew who I am!"

Not far from the castle of the Baron of Montefiascone was the luxurious summer palace of the Prince of Salerno. The Prince was seeking a bride, and hearing of the Baron's two daughters, he sent courtiers to the castle of Montefiascone.

When they arrived, one courtier stepped forward and announced:

The Prince of Salerno is coming to call,
And escort you both to his summer ball.
Tonight is the night when he will decide
Which beautiful lady shall be his bride.

Imagine the excitement of Tisbe and Clorinda! They rushed through the castle calling, "Cinderella, fetch our jewels, our perfumes, our silks! We must be the fairest of all!"

As the Prince of Salerno was preparing to leave for the Baron's castle, he lamented, "I am afraid every maiden in this kingdom wants only to marry a prince, and would do anything to snare him. But I know how to fool them."

Looking at his valet, he said, "Since we are the same size, let us exchange clothes. Then you will ride in the carriage and I will ride your horse."

And thus they galloped off to the Castle of Montefiascone.

The Prince, disguised as the valet, arrived first. He went to the kitchen door and there saw gentle Cinderella. Cinderella looked at the handsome valet and fell in love with him at first sight.

"Who are you, sweet maid?" asked the Prince.

"I am only the kitchen wench," said Cinderella with a sigh.

"Not one of the daughters of the Baron of Montefiascone? Where are they then?"

"Preparing for the arrival of the Prince of Salerno," said Cinderella.

At that moment, a great flourish of trumpets sounded.

The splendid carriage of the Prince of Salerno drew up to the castle gate. The Baron of Montefiascone and his two daughters bowed down to the ground exclaiming, "Highest of Highnesses!"

The false Prince descended from the carriage and said, "Like a bee in springtime, I seek the lily or the rose who can bring joy into my life."

The Baron beamed. "Highest of Highnesses, my daughters are the choicest blossoms of any garden!"

Cinderella, who had followed the false valet, said in a small voice, "May I come to watch the ball?"

"Back to the kitchen!" the Baron roared. Then he exclaimed, "Let us be off so the merrymaking can begin!" He helped his two daughters into the carriage of the Prince and they left for the grand ball.

Poor Cinderella went back to the kitchen and sat near the fire thinking of the handsome valet. "Will I ever see him again?" she said and sighed.

"Don't cry, Cinderella," said a voice. Out of the darkest corner of the kitchen stepped the strange beggar, this time dressed as a magician. "I have returned to take you to the ball."

He waved his hand over a pumpkin and transformed it into a golden coach. Maids then appeared to dress Cinderella in a gown sewn with gold thread, and shoes covered with diamonds and pearls.

"Is this a dream?" asked the bewildered Cinderella.

"Shh, all this is yours, but only till the stroke of midnight. Remember!" And the mysterious beggar led Cinderella to the waiting carriage.

The ball was the most spectacular event in the history of Montefiascone. All the maidens of the kingdom were there adorned in their most sumptuous gowns and most glittering jewels.

Who among them would the Prince of Salerno choose as his bride?

The Baron of Montefiascone and his two daughters did not leave the side of the false Prince for a moment. "See Your Highness," said the Baron, "there are no roses here more glorious than my daughters."

Just then a golden coach arrived, and out of it stepped the most beautiful maiden in the world.

Who could she be? Where had she come from?

The true Prince, disguised as his valet, came forward. "Something about this maiden is familiar to me," he said to himself.

Bending low, the Prince asked for the privilege of dancing with her.

And so Cinderella danced happily all evening with the handsome valet, without knowing who he really was. But at the first stroke of midnight she fled, and as she ran away, one of her slippers fell from her foot.

"What has happened? Why did she run away?" asked the true Prince, picking up the slipper.

He called to his valet. "The ball is over. Bring my carriage. Hurry so we can overtake the owner of this slipper—the maid who has stolen my heart." And they rushed off.

The mysterious beggar, hidden in the shadows, heard everything. "And now to make sure that the Prince will stop at the Baron's castle, and then. . . ."

The Prince's carriage careened through the night, when suddenly a shadow crossed the road and the startled horses turned the carriage into a ditch. Seeking help, the Prince and the valet knocked at the door of a nearby castle. How surprised they were when the Baron of Montefiascone appeared to greet them!

"Ah!" the Baron exclaimed, "the Prince has chosen one of my daughters! Tisbe! Clorinda! Come here! Cinderella, bring our best chair for His Highness!"

"May we try this slipper on your daughters?" asked the true Prince. "We are searching for its owner. She is the one the Prince will marry."

Tisbe tried first, and then Clorinda, but both screeched like wounded crows, because their feet were much, much too large.

Just then Cinderella came in, dragging the chair, and the Prince, seeing her, said, "Let us try the slipper on her, too."

"Not on the wench!" shouted the Baron. But the Prince ignored him and Cinderella tried on the slipper.

The slipper fit her foot perfectly!

"I have found you at last!" the Prince exclaimed.

"My handsome valet," said Cinderella.

"I am not a valet but the real Prince, while that man dressed as the Prince is simply my valet. Through this masquerade, I have been able to tell who is really worthy of becoming the Princess of Salerno. Now, before all of you, I hereby announce that Cinderella will become my bride, and that the marriage will take place at the Palace of Salerno."

And the Prince departed, taking Cinderella with him.

Royal guests came from every land for the wedding of the Prince and Cinderella. Even the Baron and his daughters appeared, and as they kneeled before Cinderella asking her pardon, everyone's joy was beyond description.

"Virtue always triumphs in the end," observed the mysterious beggar, who in reality was the Grand Magician of Naples and the Prince of Salerno's tutor.

For if it had not been for him, Cinderella would not have married the Prince of Salerno, and lived happily ever after.

THE END

Gioacchino Rossini (1792-1868) is one of the great Italian operatic composers of the nineteenth century. CENERENTOLA, *Rossini's Cinderella, was first performed in Rome in January 25, 1817, when he was only twenty-five. But it was not his initial effort, for he had composed his first opera at the age of nineteen. Other popular operas which Rossini wrote are* THE BARBER OF SEVILLE *and* WILLIAM TELL.

Beni Montresor grew up in Verona, Italy. He has designed for films and theater throughout Europe. In this country, he made his theatrical debut designing Gian Carlo Menotti's THE LAST SAVAGE *for the Metropolitan Opera. His books for children have received wide acclaim. His own books, including* THE WITCHES OF VENICE *and* HOUSE OF FLOWERS, HOUSE OF STARS, *have been on all the best books lists. He has won awards from* AIGA *and the Society of Illustrators. And this year, 1965, he was awarded the Caldecott Medal for the best illustrated book of the year for Beatrice de Reigners'* MAY I BRING A FRIEND?